THE
MAIL-COACH DRIVER

THE
MAIL-COACH DRIVER

by
ELIZABETH RENIER
Illustrated by Eric Stemp

HAMISH HAMILTON
LONDON

First published in Great Britain 1985
by Hamish Hamilton Children's Books
Garden House 57–59 Long Acre London WC2E 9JZ
Copyright © 1985 by Elizabeth Renier
Illustrations copyright © 1985 by Hamish Hamilton Ltd

British Library Cataloguing in Publication Data
Renier, Elizabeth
   The mail-coach driver.—(Antelope books)
   I. Title   II. Stemp, Eric
   823'.914[J]   PZ7

ISBN 0-241-11654-6

Filmset in Baskerville by
Katerprint Co. Ltd, Oxford
Printed in Great Britain at the
University Press, Cambridge

For Katie

Chapter 1

MATTHEW PICKED UP the satchel containing all his belongings and took a last look around the kitchen. His mother was putting on a brave smile, his two young sisters trying not to cry. *He* was sad, too, at leaving home, but he was eleven years old and determined to look on his new life as an adventure.

His father, coachman to Squire Travis, had died, two months ago. Now the cottage was wanted for the new coachman. Squire had found Matthew's mother a post as housekeeper where the two little girls would be welcome, but not a boy.

"Squire Travis has been very good," his mother had told Matthew, a week

ago. "He's got you a job with Sir Walter Ashby of Woodhayes."

"Where's that?" Matthew asked.

"On the way to Exeter, I believe. Still in Devonshire, anyway."

"I *am* to go as stable-lad?"

"Of course. Squire knows you're

2

good with horses, that you hoped to take your father's place one day. I expect your new employer will have a great number of horses, being a titled gentleman."

His mother, who could not read or write, had put her mark to a document promising that Matthew would remain at Woodhayes for seven years.

Now, as Matthew made for the door, she said, "You behave, and work hard and you could do very well for yourself."

Outside, in the April sunshine, a group of people had gathered to wish him Godspeed: Squire and his lady and three children; the indoor servants; the gardeners and groom and farm workers. In fact, all the people who made up the busy, cheerful life of Squire Travis's small estate.

Matthew had already said goodbye to the horses, alone in the stables, but as he walked along the lane which led to the highroad, the Squire's two hunters trotted across the paddock and kept pace with him on the other side of the fence. He gave them a final pat, turned at the corner of the lane to wave for the last time to his family. Then, running now, he went on his way.

When he reached the highroad, he sat on a bank to wait for the wagon which would take him to Woodhayes. It soon came into view, a huge vehicle with a canvas hood, drawn by eight heavy horses, their hooves raising the dust from the rutted road. Mr Yeo, the waggoner, dressed in a smock and carrying a long whip, walked alongside.

"D'you want to ride in the wagon or

walk along of me for a while?" he asked.

"I'll walk," said Matthew, and tossed his satchel into the wagon.

Mr Yeo said, "I was sorry to hear about your father. An accident, was it?"

Matthew did not want to think about that dreadful night but the waggoner looked so sympathetic, he told him what had happened.

"There was a bad storm which frightened the horses, so Father went to them. A gust of wind blew the stable door open and knocked Father off his feet. He banged his head against the drinking-trough. Squire Travis called the doctor but Father – he died the next day. Mother sometimes said Father thought more of the horses than he did of his family. It wasn't true, of course, but he *did* care about them. He was proud of them, too."

Mr Yeo scratched his chin with his thumb, making a rasping sound.

"Horses," he said, thoughtfully. "They take over your life once you start working with them. 'Tis no good me thinking I can put my feet up when I get to the end of a day's journey. Oh, no! This lot have to be fed and watered, taken to the blacksmith's when they need shoeing, made a bit of fuss of if we've had a specially hard day. Mind you, there's many that don't give a thought to their animals except how much work they can get out of them."

"I hope the coachman at Woodhayes treats his horses well."

"If not, you'll take a whip to *him*, I shouldn't wonder," Mr Yeo said, jovially. "You're a lad with plenty of spirit, I reckon."

After a while Matthew decided to

ride in the wagon. He wished the team could go faster but they were heavy horses, bred for long hours of hard pulling at a steady pace, not thoroughbreds out of a gentleman's stable. All the same, the gentry in their carriages sometimes had to give way because the huge wagon took up most of the road.

They had just passed a toll-gate, where Mr Yeo paid the charge levied for the upkeep of the road, when Matthew saw a gig coming towards them. It was

driven by a lady, with a groom beside her.

"Move out of the way, my man," she ordered. "I wish to pass."

The waggoner touched his hat respectfully. "Beggin' your pardon, ma'am, 'tis not possible. There's a deep ditch this side."

"That is your affair. Move over, I say."

The groom, looking nervous, began, "I think, m'lady . . ."

"I do not wish to hear what you think, Sanders. If this man does not move out of my way . . ." The lady flicked her whip towards Mr Yeo.

From beyond the toll-gate, a horn sounded, loud and clear.

"Mercy on us!" exclaimed Mr Yeo. "'Tis the London to Exeter mail-coach!"

The groom leaped down from his seat.

"What are you doing?" demanded his mistress.

"I'll have to back the mare into that gateway, m'lady."

"Indeed you will not. I forbid it."

The groom said anxiously, "With respect, your ladyship knows the rule. Everything must give way to the Royal Mail."

Furiously she tapped her whip against the side of the gig as it was backed into a gateway.

The horn sounded again. Peering around the canvas hood of the wagon, Matthew saw a cloud of dust. Then a coach came into view, travelling fast. It was painted maroon and black, with red wheels, and drawn by four splendid horses, bob-tailed and wearing blinkers. There were three outside passengers. At the back, a man in a red coat was blowing a long horn.

At sight of the wagon, the coachman pulled hard on his reins. Matthew braced himself, sure that the horses could not stop in time. At the last moment they veered to the right, the coachman shouting encouragement. Matthew felt a jolt. The mail-coach lurched, swayed, then steadied. With no more than a scratch on its paint-work, it passed through the gap which had defeated the lady in her gig.

Mr Yeo fanned himself with his hat. "My, that was a narrow shave!"

It was a few moments before Matthew could even speak at all. Then, "That was *wonderful*," he said in an awed voice. "He must be the cleverest coach-man in all the world."

"*One* of the cleverest," said the wag-goner, urging his team forward. "There's many like that among the mail-coach men. Lords of the road, they are."

"Why did even the lady have to get out of the way?"

"Because the Royal Mail has the right of the road. Even the toll-gates have to be opened as soon as the toll-keeper hears the horn. Mail-coaches don't pay tolls like the rest of us."

"Why not?" Matthew persisted. "Why are they so important?"

Mr Yeo blew out his cheeks. "You're like all lads, always asking questions. The Royal Mail carries letters and parcels and important documents all over the British Isles. Day or night, whatever the weather, there are always mail-coaches travelling along the King's highway. And it's the rule of the Post Office that they have to be on time. They can be a nuisance to the rest of us but there's no denying they're the cream of the coaching world, the mail-coach drivers."

For the rest of the journey, Matthew was lost in a dream. Instead of the broad backs of the eight plodding wagon horses, he saw four splendid creatures at full gallop. One hand was clenched as if holding reins, the other clasped a long-handled whip. He wore a caped coat and tall hat. He was driving his team through the night, braving all weathers and dangers to get the mail through on time. He was no longer a stable-lad, but a "lord of the road".

He was still lost in his dream when the wagon creaked to a halt.

"This is Woodhayes," said Mr Yeo.

They had stopped beside iron gates set in a high wall which stretched as far as Matthew could see in each direction. The gates were padlocked.

"I reckon there must be another entrance you're supposed to use," the waggoner said. "We passed a lane a little way back. Best try that. D'you want me to come with you?"

Matthew wanted to say "Yes", because he suddenly felt tired and hungry and a little scared. Instead, he shouldered his satchel and answered jauntily, "No, thanks. I'll manage."

A short way up the lane was a green door set in the wall which seemed to go on for ever. This door, also, was locked. Squire Travis's gates were never locked and everybody used the same way in.

There was a rusty bell-pull beside the door. Matthew tugged at it and heard a bell clang, startling some pigeons which clattered noisily from the trees.

Presently the door was opened by a thin, elderly man with a fuzz of white whiskers.

"Well, what do you want?" he demanded in a crotchety voice.

"Please, sir, my name's Matthew Hardacre. I've come to work for Sir Walter Ashby as stable-lad."

The man said, even more crossly, "No stable-lad wanted here. Only three horses, looked after by the coachman and groom."

As the door was about to close, Matthew said urgently, "It was all arranged by Squire Travis. My mother put her mark to a paper."

The old man tugged at his whiskers. "What did you say your name was?"

When Matthew repeated it, the man said, "You must be the new garden-boy."

"No, sir," said Matthew anxiously. "Stable-lad."

The old man grabbed Matthew and pulled him inside. "Garden-boy is what you've come as, and no argument. My name's Mr Jobling. I'm Head Gardener here, and worked to the bone since that fool of an under-gardener fell off a ladder and broke his leg."

Matthew, trying to wriggle free, protested. "I don't know anything about gardening. It's horses I'm used to. Squire Travis said . . ."

"I don't care a donkey's tail what your Squire said, *or* how many marks your mother made. You've come as garden-boy and that's what you'll be. And not another word out of you. *Understand?*"

Chapter 2

AFTER TWO WEEKS at Woodhayes, Matthew had almost forgotten his dream of becoming a mail-coach driver. Mr Jobling kept him at work from first light until supper-time, with only a half-hour break at midday. It was such boring work, too – hoeing, weeding, washing clay flower-pots, sweeping the paths. The only time he entered the stable was to collect manure and add it to the steaming pile beside the potting-shed, and at night to reach his bed, a straw mattress on the floor of the little room next to the hay-loft, which he shared with an old ginger cat. He had not even met Sir Walter or Lady Ashby.

"A garden-boy is not allowed to be seen by his employers," Mr Jobling said. "It is one of my rules."

Matthew was jabbing at a tough dandelion root between the stones of the terrace when a window opened above him and a duster was shaken out, a duster full of feathers. They tickled Matthew's nose and made him sneeze.

"Sorry," said a cheerful voice. "I didn't know you were there."

"I wish I wasn't," said Matthew, crossly. "I wish I was anywhere but here."

Kitty, a housemaid, who was thirteen and the only young person he had seen at Woodhayes, said, "Oh dear, you don't sound very happy this morning."

"I'm not. I *hate* it here."

"It's a good place to work. Plenty to eat, a comfortable bed, and her lady-

ship leaves us alone to get on with our jobs."

"You're lucky! Mr Jobling's always finding fault with me." Matthew jabbed again at the dandelion root. "I didn't come to Woodhayes to be a garden-boy. I expected to work with horses, to be a stable-lad. And nobody talks to me, except you."

"No wonder you're down in the dumps, then," Kitty said, sympathetically. "Cheer up, though, it'll soon be time for your noonday piece. Pork pie today, big slices. I saw Cook cutting them up."

Matthew's spirits rose a little. "I shall take mine to the meadow where the horses are. At least *they're* glad of my company."

When the stable clock struck twelve, Matthew flung down the hoe, collected his pie and took it to the far meadow. The two carriage horses and the grey pony were beneath an oak tree near the wall. He pulled some long grass and fed it to them.

Suddenly, he heard the distant tan-tara of a horn. Surely it was the same horn he had heard on his journey to Woodhayes, when the mail-coach so narrowly missed running into Mr Yeo's wagon?

A branch of the oak tree overhung the wall. Matthew climbed up quickly and found he had a splendid view. To his left, the road disappeared amongst trees for a short distance. On the other side of the wood was a steep hill.

The horn sounded again, clear and demanding. Then the mail-coach came over the brow of the hill. Travelling fast, it was soon lost to sight in the

wood. A few moments later it emerged, the horses at full stretch. Matthew almost fell off the branch in his excitement as the coach swept past in a swirl of dust and colour and noise.

Afterwards, all was quiet. Dust settled on the road. Rabbits came out of their burrows. The stable clock struck the half-hour.

Matthew ran all the way back

but Mr Jobling was there before him.

"You're three minutes late," the gardener grumbled. "*And* your work's not been done properly. There are several dandelion roots just under the dining-room window."

For Matthew, now, there was something to look forward to – a few moments of excitement to set against the boredom and homesickness. Each noonday he climbed to the overhanging branch. Each day he heard the horn, summoning the toll-keeper to open the gate. Then the coach appeared, travelling swiftly down the hill, through the wood and along the road beside the high wall of Woodhayes. He noted every detail, the lettering on the door, the signs that looked like stars on the side panels, a blunderbuss beside the horn in the compartment at the back where the guard had charge of the mail-box.

On some days there would be different horses but the coachman and guard were always the same. Although Matthew took care they did not see him, for fear he should get into further trouble with Mr Jobling, he came to look upon them almost as his friends.

One morning there was a gale. The oak tree creaked and strained against the wind. Twigs and leaves whirled along the road. The grass looked as if a giant hand was smoothing it flat.

A tremendous gust almost made Matthew lose his grip. There was a loud crack, then a rending sound which set his teeth on edge. Between the swaying branches he saw that a tree had fallen across the road, right in the path of the mail-coach.

"I must warn the driver," said Matthew, aloud. "I *must*."

He looked down at the deep ditch at the base of the wall. It would be a dangerous jump. But if he did not attempt it, there would surely be a terrible accident to the mail-coach.

Climbing along the branch as far as he dared, he hung by his hands, counted three, then let go. He landed with a splash in the ditch, scrambled up the bank and raced along the road to the uprooted tree. Forcing his way between the tangled branches, he ran on to the wood. It was so dark amongst the trees he thought the coachman might not see him. However loud he shouted he would not be heard against the turmoil of the storm.

He had just come out from the trees when, in a sudden lull, he heard the horn. A few moments later the coach appeared on the brow of the hill. Matthew stood in the middle of the road, waving his arms wildly and yelling at the top of his voice. The coachman leaned back, pulling hard on the reins. The horses were almost on top of Matthew before he leaped out of their way.

"You young varmint!" shouted the coachman, flourishing his whip. "I'll have the hide off you for—"

"There's a tree down," Matthew called. "It's right across the road."

"I don't see any tree. If you're lying, boy . . ."

"*I'm not! I'm not!* It's on the far side of the wood. I saw it fall and ran as fast as I could."

"Up with you, then, and show us."

The coachman leaned down to help

Matthew on to the step. He could hardly believe what was happening. He was actually riding on the mail-coach, even if it *was* only on the step and such a short distance.

When the coachman saw the fallen tree, he puffed out his cheeks. "It will certainly need every man's hand to shift that."

The male passengers, together with the coachman and guard and Matthew, pushed and pulled but with no success. The tree rocked a little, then fell back across the road.

"I'll have to use the horses," the coachman said.

Two were taken from the coach and the traces fastened round a strong branch. The splendid pair strained against their collars. Everyone cheered as the tree was heaved on to the verge.

"Thank you, gentlemen," called the coachman, swiftly untying the traces. "Back to your seats, now, if you please."

When he and the guard had put the horses to the coach again, he tossed a coin to Matthew.

"Here, boy. Take this for your trouble. We could have had a nasty accident but for your warning."

In seconds the coach was on its way, the horses' manes streaming out in the wind, the outside passengers clutching their hats.

Matthew stood alone in the empty road. Everything had happened so swiftly he could almost believe it had been a dream. But *there* was the tree on the verge and here was the coin in his hand. A sixpence. *A whole sixpence!*

He, Matthew Hardacre, eleven years old and only a garden-boy, had saved the Royal Mail from being overturned, people and horses hurt, killed even, and been rewarded by his hero.

His dream was reborn. Some day, somehow, he *would* become a mail-coach driver.

"How did you get back?" asked Kitty, taking in some washing before Matthew swept up the debris of the previous day's storm.

He had told Kitty of his adventure after making her promise she would keep it a secret.

"I found some ivy with thick stems and climbed up that. Then I wriggled along the top of the wall to the oak tree."

"You were very brave," said Kitty. "You might have been killed."

Matthew was pleased with her praise

but he said, casually, "I had to save the mail-coach, if I'm to become . . ."

"Yes?" she prompted as he broke off.

He shrugged. "Oh, nothing." Not even to Kitty did he dare tell of his dream. It would sound so silly and impossible.

"Did you get into trouble for being late back?"

"No. I was lucky. Mr Jobling didn't even notice, *or* the state I was in from the ditch. The wind had blown down some netting in the chicken-run and a fox had got in and killed six hens."

"So *that's* why there are so many in the larder. Maybe you'll be having chicken-pie for your noonday piece tomorrow!"

On Sunday evening Matthew was in the meadow with the horses when he heard Kitty calling him. She was carrying a basket covered with a cloth, and a milk-can.

"Lady Ashby asked me to take some broth and eggs to an old woman who lives on her own in a cottage beyond the wood. I told her ladyship you'd be glad of an outing and she said you can come with me if you like."

"Oh, yes, please," said Matthew, delighted at the idea.

Kitty's cheeks were a little pink as she said, "As a matter of fact, I didn't want to go alone, not through the wood, I mean."

As they set off, Matthew brandished a stick brought down by the gale.

"Ho, ho, ho, you wolves!" he cried. "I'm not afraid of you."

"There aren't really any wolves, are there?" Kitty asked, anxiously.

"I was only pretending. Shall I carry the milk-can?"

Matthew was wearing the suit his mother had made for him to wear to church on Sundays, and his good boots. Kitty, too, was in her Sunday best. Birds were singing and there were primroses in the hedgerows. Matthew wanted to run and leap about but remembered just in time he was carrying the broth.

They stayed a long while at the old woman's, Kitty tidying the cottage and Matthew chopping wood for her fire. It was dusk when they left.

At the edge of the wood, Kitty said, "It's so *dark*, Matthew, like a black cave ready to swallow us up."

"It's only trees."

"Someone might be hiding among the trees, waiting to pounce on us. I

wish we'd brought a lantern and you
hadn't left your stick at the cottage."

"Who'd want to pounce on *us*?" said

Matthew, scornfully, but to please Kitty he searched for another heavy stick.

He was groping in the undergrowth when he heard padding footsteps further inside the wood.

Kitty clutched at his arm. "What was that?"

"Only a badger, I expect. This wood must be full of wild animals – badgers, foxes, deer. They won't hurt you."

The footsteps came nearer. Two eyes stared at them out of the darkness. They were not the eyes of badger or deer or fox. More like a cat's, thought Matthew, but much, much bigger. Then came a low, menacing growl.

Kitty's fingers dug into Matthew's arm, as they clung on to each other in fright.

"Let's make a noise. Animals are

scared of loud noises," said Matthew.

He rattled the lid of the milk-can. Kitty put down her basket and clapped her hands. When they stopped to listen, there was silence.

"That did the trick," said Matthew, jubilantly. "It *must* have been a badger." Then, remembering the eyes, he added, jokingly, "Or even just the ginger cat from the stable."

All the same, he was as relieved as Kitty when they were safely back inside the high, protective walls of Woodhayes.

Chapter 3

MONDAY WAS A bad day. Matthew broke several flower-pots and overturned a wheelbarrow full of fresh manure on Mr Jobling's carefully prepared seed-bed. The gardener threatened to report him to Sir Walter. Even worse, he made Matthew work through his noonday break, which meant he missed seeing the mail-coach. That night he was so tired and homesick he did not even bother to take off his clothes or boots. With the ginger cat curled up beside him, he fell immediately asleep.

He woke in the night, with a feeling that something was wrong. The horses were restless, the yard-dog rattling its chain. The ginger cat was no longer beside him.

Quietly he got up and crept down the ladder. It was dark in the stable. There was the smell of fear in the air, and fresh blood.

Matthew spoke softly to the horses. "It'll only be rats at the corn-bins. I reckon the cat has just killed one."

But the ginger cat hunted rats and mice every night. Nothing in that to alarm the horses, or the yard-dog.

Matthew felt around for a hay-fork, then took a lantern from its hook and groped for the tinder-box. As the lantern flared into light, the cat streaked past, her fur on end.

Matthew's heart beat fast, his hands were clammy, as he moved stealthily along the passage beside the loose-boxes. He had reached the pile of bed-ding straw when he heard a sound which made him hold his breath. From

just ahead of him but beyond the flick-
ering light of the lantern, the sound
came again – the low, menacing growl
he and Kitty had heard last night. He
saw the gleam of eyes, the same eyes
which had stared at him out of the
darkness of the wood. The animal came
within the lantern's range. It was huge,
tawny-coloured, like a nightmare copy
of the ginger cat. Its long tail swished

angrily. In its mouth was a freshly-killed chicken.

The hay-fork shook in Matthew's hand. In his fright, he dropped the lantern. As it fell, the glass broke. The

flame found the straw, and flared into orange light. The beast snarled, then turned, seeking a way of escape. With one bound it reached the top of the stable wall, squeezed through a gap beneath the roof and disappeared.

For a few seconds, Matthew was too scared to move. Behind him, the horses kicked at the sides of their stalls.

Suddenly realising the danger, Matthew grabbed a sack and tried to beat out the flames. When that failed, he ran for the water buckets. As the fire died down, he raked away the damp, smouldering straw.

He thought he had it under control, but it flared up again. Shouting, he ran into the yard. The dog was barking wildly. A bedroom window opened and the coachman called sleepily, "What's all the noise about?"

"*Fire!*" yelled Matthew. "*Fire in the stables! Come quickly!*"

Orange-red flames lit up roof and stalls. Smoke billowed above the loose-boxes. The horses plunged and reared, snorting their terror.

Matthew freed the two carriage horses, leaping aside as they jostled each other in their wild rush to escape. The bolt of the pony's stall was rusty. Almost choking with smoke, Matthew pulled it back at last. As he ran into the yard he saw a flash of white. The coachman, in his nightshirt, sprawled on the cobbles, knocked down by the fleeing pony.

Roused by the hubbub, the indoor

servants scattered as the carriage horses bolted headlong from the yard. The dog kept up its frenzied barking.

Matthew found Kitty beside him, a coat over her nightdress.

"We ought to be fetching water," she shouted, to make herself heard.

Matthew had his first sight of Sir Walter, a tall man with stooping shoulders, in a purple dressing-gown and tasselled nightcap.

"The girl's right," he said. "Quickly, now, form up in line."

When the water tank and horse-trough had been emptied, Matthew and Kitty were sent to fill buckets from the fish pond. Through it all, Mr Jobling could be heard grumbling.

"Them dratted horses! They'll trample all over the garden. 'Twill be a proper shambles in the morning."

At length the flames died down. The horses were caught and stabled in another block. Matthew and Kitty, exhausted, sat on the mounting-block.

"How did the fire start?" she asked.

When Matthew told her, she said, "It

must have been the same animal that was in the wood last night. What *can* it be?"

"I don't know. I've never seen anything like it before. It was *enormous*."

"You *must* have been scared."

"Yes, I was," he admitted. "That's why I dropped the lantern, setting fire to the straw."

"So it was *you* started the fire. I might have known that." Mr Jobling's voice brought them to their feet.

"I didn't mean to," Matthew protested.

"You didn't mean to! Not when you're fully dressed and with your boots on, in the middle of the night. Don't you lie to me, boy, *or* to Sir Walter when he questions you about this night's mischief. You'll be sent packing, I don't doubt, and good riddance. In all my

born days I never had to put up with
such a useless bungle-head."

He stumped off, tugging angrily at
his whiskers.

"How *can* he think I did it on purpose, risking the horses' lives?" cried
Matthew.

"And your own," said Kitty, backing
him up. "Besides, you've lost everything but what you're wearing, haven't
you?"

Matthew looked at the burnt-out
stable. The roof had fallen in, taking
with it the little room where he slept.

"I didn't have much," he said, dejectedly, "but it's all gone now. And if I'm sent back, without even my Sunday suit, what will my mother say?"

Kitty put a hand on his shoulder. "It won't be like that. You've only to tell Sir Walter the truth."

"That I saw a huge wild animal with a chicken in its mouth? He'll say it was only the fox that raided the hen-run. Nobody'll believe me, Kitty, except you."

Matthew's eyes were watering from the smoke, and from tears. He left Kitty and made for the potting-shed and spent the rest of the night there, hidden under one of the benches. Except for the day his father died, he had never felt so miserable in his life.

Next morning, Matthew was summoned to the library. The footman who was to show him the way, said scorn-fully, "You can't appear before Sir Walter like that. You look worse than a scarecrow."

"I can't help it. I lost my best suit in the fire."

The footman showed no sympathy. "You can at least take off those filthy boots. Her ladyship is very particular about the carpets."

Matthew tugged off his boots and tried to pull his trousers down to hide his dirty legs as he followed the footman across the hall.

Sir Walter was standing by the window, drumming his fingers on the sill.

"Your name is Matthew Hardacre?" he asked.

Matthew was so nervous, his "Yes, sir" was no more than a whisper.

Sir Walter cupped a hand behind his

ear. "Speak up, boy, my hearing isn't good nowadays. I am told you work here as garden-boy although I don't remember having seen you about the place."

Matthew made an effort to speak up. "Mr Jobling said I was to keep out of sight whenever you or her ladyship came into the garden."

"How very odd! I think he would have us believe the paths are swept and flower-beds weeded by little gnomes who arrive in the night. Well, boy, don't you think that's funny?"

"Yes, sir," Matthew ventured, not knowing what to make of his employer.

"Laugh, then." When Matthew did so, Sir Walter said, "Good, excellent. Not many people appreciate my jokes. Now, let us be serious. Jobling tells me he suspects you started the fire last night. Did you?"

"No, sir. At least, not on purpose."

Sir Walter drummed his fingers again, harder this time. "Either you did or you did not. Because I encourage you to laugh at my joke does not mean you can take liberties. Tell me exactly what happened – *exactly*."

When Matthew had finished his

story, Sir Walter exclaimed, "Bless my soul, it must have been the lioness!"

"*Lioness?*"

"You may well look astonished. On my way back from Exeter yesterday I heard that one had escaped from a travelling menagerie and I intended warning everybody. Probably the fact that it had eaten well on my chickens stopped it attacking you or the horses but it must have been a very frightening experience for you." Sir Walter looked down at Matthew from his great height. "Now I come to think of it, I was given some other news at The Swan Inn – about a boy who saved the Royal Mail from a nasty accident just outside my grounds. I wonder if you know any-thing about that?"

Suddenly Matthew felt he could trust this odd but seemingly kindly man. He told Sir Walter about his noonday climb up the oak tree to watch the mail-coach pass each day.

"I see," said Sir Walter. "You know, when I was a young man, I used to bribe the coachman on the Exeter to Taunton road to let me handle the ribbons – that's what they call the reins. I remember the thrill of driving a four-in-hand, the bugle playing a merry tune and the roof passengers singing. That was a stage-coach. The Royal Mail has stricter rules."

"And a horn, sir, not a bugle," said Matthew, greatly daring.

"True, true, but they both make a cheerful sound." Sir Walter's fingers were tapping again. This time it sounded like a tune. "It was a long time ago but some incidents I remember most clearly – the narrow escape we had when a donkey lay down in the road and rolled just ahead of the coach; the night a bull charged at the lamps and we all had to hold on for dear life. I remember, too, the feel of the ribbons between my fingers, the sense of power." Sir Walter sighed. "It is not nearly so enjoyable to be driven in one's own carriage."

"You *understand*," said Matthew, as if he were talking to a friend instead of his employer.

Sir Walter looked vague. "Understand? Oh, about the fire, you mean?"

It was not what Matthew had meant but he had to let it pass because the next moment Sir Walter said, "You will be rewarded for your bravery and prompt action last night, in saving my horses. Now, what shall it be? Ah, I know. How would you like a ride on the mail-coach?"

Matthew could only stare. A reward, instead of dismissal! And *what* a reward!

Sir Walter laughed. "You look like a fish gulping in air but it would seem you like the idea. I will arrange it. Now, back to your work, boy, and try to make more effort to please Mr Jobling. He is an excellent gardener, he can teach you a great deal."

As Matthew made for the door he felt as if he was walking on a cloud instead of the unfamiliar softness of a carpet.

Chapter 4

SIR WALTER THOUGHT the lioness would have been frightened by the fire and unlikely to return to Woodhayes. Even so, everybody kept close to the house for the next few days.

Matthew was dead-heading daffodils when Kitty appeared, carrying a parcel.

"See what I have for you! A new suit and boots for you to wear when you ride on the mail-coach tomorrow."

"*Tomorrow?*" Matthew's voice rose with excitement.

"It's all arranged. You're to wait at the end of the lane for Mr Askew, the carrier. He'll take you to The Swan Inn where you board the mail-coach. Sir

Walter has paid your fare to the next post-house – about ten miles. He says you're sure to get a lift back with a carter or waggoner." Kitty produced some coins from her apron pocket. "These are for tips."

"Only gentry give tips," Matthew said.

Kitty laughed. "That's what you'll be tomorrow, gentry. You mind you behave," she added, sounding almost like his mother. "I shall want to hear all about your adventure when you get back."

It was a fine, breezy morning when Matthew set off along the lane leading to the highway. Several vehicles passed by while he waited, and some riders on horseback. After what seemed to him a long time, he saw the carrier's cart, piled high with boxes and barrels.

Mr Askew moved an old blunderbuss from the plank which served as seat.

"I brought that along in case I got a sight of the wild animal that escaped from a menagerie," he explained, "but she's been caught this morning, so I've heard."

"That's good news," said Matthew, and he told the carrier of his two encounters with the lioness.

At The Swan Inn bread and cheese and a mug of cider had been ordered for him by Sir Walter.

"Can I watch the horses being harnessed?" he asked the innkeeper.

"So long as you don't get in the way. Only five minutes is allowed for changing the teams."

Matthew went into the yard. A boy little older than he was came out of a stable, leading a piebald. Matthew watched enviously.

Suddenly he had an idea which almost made him choke on his cider. This was his chance to escape – from the work he hated, from Mr Jobling's continual fault-finding, the dullness and loneliness of his life at Woodhayes. He had money in his pocket for he had brought his sixpence as well as the coins for tips. His absence would not be noticed until tomorrow. By that time he could be in Exeter where he could surely find employment at one of the

coaching inns. He would be part of the world where he truly belonged, the world of horses and the Royal Mail.

The horse-keeper called, "There's the horn. Out with the horses, quickly, now."

Matthew's heart was beating fast as he followed the team into the road. The mail-coach came into view, clattering through the village. As soon as it stopped, the tired horses were unharnessed and led away. The fresh team was backed into place while the guard

delivered his mail-bag. Matthew climbed
on to the seat beside the coachman.
Then they were off, the horn blaring its
warning.

The coach lurched and swayed. At
the first bend, Matthew would have
fallen off if the coachman had not grabbed him.

"Hold fast, boy! Brace your feet
against the front board."

The coachman had to shout to make
himself heard above the pounding
hooves, the rumble and creak of the
wheels, the crack of the long whip

above the horses' backs. The wind whistled past Matthew's ears. Trees and buildings flashed by. With a tan-tara on the horn, they overtook a gentleman's carriage, then a gig.

The coachman glanced at Matthew. "Enjoying it?"

"Yes, oh yes!"

The coachman looked at him more closely. "I've seen you before. I know, you're the lad who warned us about the fallen tree."

"That's right," said Matthew, thril-led that his hero remembered him.

"I didn't recognise you at first, you're looking so smart today. Not like . . ." He broke off, looking worried. "The team's nervous. Something's wrong."

His attention was entirely on his horses. It was Matthew who saw the animal running across a field alongside

the road – a big animal, tawny-
coloured, keeping pace with the coach.

"The lioness!" Matthew shouted. "She
must have escaped again. She's making
for that gate! She'll come out in the
road."

The coachman hauled on the reins.

"Have your gun ready!" he yelled to
the guard.

As the lioness neared the gate, Matthew heard shouts and barking. Two men were running across the field, one almost dragged along by a fierce-looking dog on a leash. A woman

passenger screamed as the lioness bounded through the gateway. It leaped at the offside lead horse. The horse reared, trying to fight off the grasping claws with its forefeet.

As the guard took aim, the men rushed into the road, shouting. *"Don't shoot. Don't shoot!"*

The mastiff was let loose. It made straight for the lioness which turned, snarling, to face its attacker.

One of the men threw a hunk of raw meat on the road. The lioness growled menacingly at the dog, then took up the meat and carried it to a barn beside the gate. The man leashed the dog and moved cautiously forward, a lasso in his hand.

The frightened horses had tangled themselves in their traces. At any moment they could overturn the coach.

The guard leaped down and ran to
them. For a moment Matthew hesi-
tated. Then he, too, scrambled from his
high perch.

"Good lad," called the guard. "Can
you hold the piebald?"

"I'll try."

Matthew clung on, feeling as if his
arms would crack. The coachman
joined them and set about freeing the
injured horse. Matthew's joyful adventure became a nightmare world of

kicking hooves and bared teeth; of screams and shouts and frenzied barking. And, sounding very close, a roar from the lioness as the barn door was banged shut.

At last the traces were straightened, the horses under control.

"Come on, lad," ordered the coachman, running back while the guard held the leaders' heads.

"What about the horse the lioness attacked?" asked Matthew, worried because there was blood on its neck.

"He's not badly hurt. He'll keep going until the next post-house. They'll attend to him there."

As soon as the coachman had the reins, the guard hurried to his seat at the back. When they were on their way again, the coachman said, "That was a bit of excitement you didn't expect, lad, but it's all in a day's work for us. Run-away horses, broken axles, hold-ups by highwaymen . . . Come snow or floods, fallen trees or even wild animals on the road, you *must* drive on. A lot of people depend on the Royal Mail and you can't let them down."

Matthew was silent, thinking over the coachman's words. "*You* must drive on," he had said. "*You* can't let them down."

It was almost as if he knew about Matthew's dream, was sure that one day Matthew *would* be a mail-coach driver. He had said something else, too, about people *depending* on the Royal Mail.

Unimportant as he was, Matthew suddenly realised that there were people even now who depended on him. Sir Walter, who had given him this day's treat. His mother, who expected him to carry out the promise she had made when she put her mark to a piece of paper, even if she had misunderstood about his being a stable-lad. Kitty, who was his friend and would want to hear all about this day's adventure.

He could not run away. For the next seven years he would have to put aside his dream, learn to be a gardener. But one day . . .

The guard's horn, blaring out its demand to a toll-keeper for the gate to be opened, brought Matthew's thoughts back to the present. There was still the rest of today, to be enjoyed to the full

and remembered on the bad days when work was at its most boring and Mr Jobling's tongue as sharp as a pruning-knife.

News of the lioness' attack on the mail-coach spread quickly. For once, Matthew was the centre of attention. Even Mr Jobling listened to his story, although afterwards he said grumpily, "Everyone else may think you're a little hero. I still consider you're a useless bungle-head and that's what I shall tell Sir Walter."

So that Matthew thought he was in for trouble when he was again sent for by his employer.

He was sure of it when Sir Walter said, "Jobling tells me he is very dissatisfied with your work."

"I do try, sir, but . . ."

"On the other hand," he said, cutting

him short, "you are undoubtedly skilled at handling horses. I heard that you helped control the team when the lioness attacked the mail-coach."

"I've been used to horses all my life, sir," said Matthew, in the hope that this time Sir Walter *would* understand. "My father was coachman to Squire Travis. I thought I'd be taking his place when he got too old."

"Indeed? Is that what you *wanted* to do?"

"Yes, sir."

"Then it is no wonder you are next to useless as a garden-boy."

Sir Walter sounded so stern that Matthew felt sure he was about to be dismissed. He might just as well have run away while he had the chance.

Sir Walter drummed his fingers on his desk. "The innkeeper at The Swan

mentioned that he can do with another stable-lad. It seems you would fit *that* job very well. If your mother agrees, I am prepared to recommend you and to free you from your bond."

Matthew's mouth gaped open in astonishment.

Sir Walter was laughing. "The gaping fish act again, I see. Well, boy what do you say?"

"*Thank you*, sir. It's very kind of you."

"Kind? To rid myself of a 'useless bungle-head?' You are aware that is what Mr Jobling calls you?"

"Yes, sir. But I have tried, truly I have."

"Then you must try a little harder, in your new job, mustn't you? And so prove that Mr Jobling is not entirely right."

That noonday, as Matthew sat astride the branch, he shouted a halloo as the mail-coach came out of the wood.

The coachman and guard looked up.
The coachman saluted Matthew with
his whip. The guard blew a tantara on
his horn. It was as if they knew already
that he would soon be joining them,
helping to get the Royal Mail through
on time, and that one day *he* would be
driving the mail-coach, one of the
"lords of the road".

Author's Note

Although slightly altered to suit this story, the incident of the lioness attacking the mail-coach is true. It happened in 1816 to the Exeter mail not far from Andover. The horse, called Pomegranate, was later sold to the menagerie and went on show as "the horse that fought a lion".